COWBOY JOSÉ

SUSAN MIDDLETON ELYA

Illustrations by TIM RAGLIN

G. P. Putnam's Sons ■ New York

To a rodeo-loving Nebraska family:
Patrick, Mary, Gayle, and Larry. —S. M. E.

For Cowboy Stan on the High Lonesome. —T. R.

Text copyright © 2005 by Susan Middleton Elya.

Illustrations copyright © 2005 by Tim Raglin.

Published simultaneously in Canada. Manufactured in China by South China Printing Co. Ltd.

Designed by Gunta Alexander. Text set Cheltenham.

The art was done in watercolor and colored pencil on Strathmore illustration board.

Library of Congress Cataloging-in-Publication Data

Elya, Susan Middleton, 1955–   Cowboy José / Susan Middleton Elya ; illustrated by Tim Raglin.   p. cm.

Summary: A poor cowboy enters a rodeo to win a date from a pretty señorita, but afterwards wonders if he should spend his winnings on the girl, who is only interested in the money, or on his trusty horse, whose encouragement helped him win.

[1. Cowboys—Fiction. 2. Horses—Fiction. 3. Rodeos—Fiction. 4. Greed—Fiction. 5. Stories in rhyme.]

I. Raglin, Tim, ill. II. Title.   PZ8.3.E514Cow 2005   [E]—dc22   2003026636   ISBN 0-399-23570-1

1 3 5 7 9 10 8 6 4 2

First Impression

Glossary

Adiós (ah DYOCE) good-bye

Bien hecho (BYEHN EH choe) well done

Bonita (boe NEE tah) pretty

Brazo (BRAH soe) arm

Bronco (BRONE koe) wild horse

Buena suerte (BWEH nah SWEHR teh) good luck

Caballo (kah BAH yoe) horse

Canciones (kahn SYONE ehs) songs

Cita (SEE tah) date, appointment

Cuero (KWEH roe) leather

Dinero (dee NEH roe) money

Feo (FEH oe) ugly

Fuerte (FWEHR teh) strong

La (LAH) the

Lazo (LAH soe) lasso

Loco (LOE koe) crazy

Maracas (mah RAH kahs) rhythm instrument
made of dried gourds

Mucho dinero (MOO choe dee NEH roe) much money

Payaso (pah YAH soe) clown

Pecho (PEH choe) chest

Pobre (POE breh) poor

Puerta (PWEHR tah) gate

Puesta de sol (PWEHS tah DEH SOLE) sunset

Rico (RREE koe) rich

Rincón (rreen KONE) corner

Rodeo (rroe DEH oe) rodeo

Sí (SEE) yes

Sombrero (sohm BREH roe) big hat

Su tronco (SOO TRONE koe) his middle

Un, Una (OON, OO nah) a, an

Un poco (OON POE koe) a little

Vacas (VAH kahs) cows

Vacíos (vah SEE oce) empty

Vaquero (vah KEH roe) cowboy

Meet a real cowboy, José, the **vaquero**.

He wears cowboy clothes, like boots made of **cuero**.

He rides his horse, Feo, who's sturdy and kind.

"José, hop on up. We've got cattle to find."

Caballo and cowboy—their friendship is strong.

They ride 'cross the prairie and belt out a song.

They sing **canciones**. José plays **maracas**.

"Get along, little dogies, get along, little **vacas**."

But one day, while singing, they see a new gal.

She smiles at José from the OK Corral.

Her name is Rosita. She's pretty—**bonita**.

He sure wants to ask for a date—**una cita**.

But she likes nice things
that cost **mucho dinero**.
She'd rather go out
with a **wealthy vaquero**.

"I need some dancing,"
she says, "and a dinner."
He looks in his wallet.
It couldn't be thinner.

José is so **pobre**,
   he hasn't got money!
He tells the gal,
   "Money ain't everything, honey."

He tips his big hat,
   his cowboy **sombrero**.
How could he *ever* be
   her rich **vaquero**?

He stands there a-poutin' until his pal Feo

says, "Why don't you enter the cowboy **rodeo**?

"The prize is a big pile of money—**dinero**—
and, gee, if you win, you'll be one rich **vaquero**!

"José," Feo says, "you could ride that horse, Loco.
You need to hang on just a little—**un poco**!"

Hang on to a **bronco**?
José begins moping.
He takes out his **lazo**
and practices roping.

"Rosita will see that you're strong;
you are **fuerte**.
And here! Take my shoe!
It's good luck—**buena suerte**."

José cries, "I'll enter!" He gets into line.
He'll ride the wild **bronco**! His horse trots behind.

Then Loco bucks one guy. The second is thrown.

The third one falls off in the corner—**rincón**.

A clown hurries over, the cowboy **payaso**.

His trick saves the rider, who's broken his **brazo**.

Our cowboy gulps hard and steps up to face Loco.

"José, are you scared?" Feo asks.

"¡Sí, un poco!"

He jumps on the **bronco**.

The **puerta** swings open.

The eight-second bell—
can he make it? He's hopin'.

"Don't blow this, **vaquero!**" yells pushy Rosita.

"You'll win me some money if you want a **cita**!"

José grips the horse at his middle—**su tronco**.

His legs squeeze the sides of the wild bucking **bronco**.

The others give up after several good tries.
José lasted longest, so he wins first prize!

The crowd yells, "Good job!" "Well done!" and "¡Bien hecho!"

José takes a bow. Feo puffs out his **pecho**.

Rosita runs over.
"My wealthy **vaquero**,
    you're rich—oh, so **rico**!
I'll spend **your dinero**!"

José eyes the gal
    and then looks back at Feo.
One yelled and one helped him
    while at the **rodeo**.

"Rosita," he says.
"You're just not my choosin'.
I want one who cares
    if I'm winnin' or losin'.

"¡Adiós!" José calls
to good-looking Rosita.
He looks at old Feo.
"Will you be my **cita**?"

The horse and the cowboy both tie on their bibs,

then sit down to dinner at Hank's House of Ribs.

José licks his fingers and Feo licks his bowl . . .

then they ride toward the sunset—**la puesta de sol**.